THE
DOZERS
ARE HERE
by
Marie Nara

To order additional copies of this book, contact:
Xlibris
844-714-8691
www.Xlibris.com
Orders@Xlibris.com

ISBN: Softcover 978-1-6698-6340-3
EBook 978-1-6698-6339-7

Print information available on the last page

Rev. date: 01/19/2023

I am a wild dog, a dog. The vast grasslands are my home. Here we roam and forage, play and sleep. Pure joy, I call it. In days gone by, I got my wish. Never solo, but in packs of at least five to ten dogs as is ideal. Lopping and lolloping and just having fun. My mama said that in her youth, she traversed these greens in the company of up fifty wild dogs! I can only imagine.

Mama is no more. Nor are any of her company or mine. Mama seems to have seen it coming. I didn't. At the height of bliss, I saw no evil.

Who killed my mother, my father, and my siblings? Who silenced the hyena? I hated his laugh, but now I dream of it. A warthog here, a hedgehog there, and maybe a gazelle. That's all I see. I avoided our intruders for a long time, but they've come too close on every front and there is no escaping. We're all bewildered No one seems at ease. With our serenity gone, no one eats or sleeps: no grazing, no browsing, no hunting. How can we when our serenity has been so abused?

Bulldozers, earthmovers, and rumblers moved in without a care. They are clearing every inch of the jungle. The din is unbearable, plus the aftermath and desolation. We have nothing and nowhere to forage.

Many years ago, a puppy joined my family. There were five of us, but the newcomer was different. He looked my age but was rotund and not interested in hunting like the rest of us.

"Chubby isn't one of us," my mother said. "He's lost and we must help him back to his home."

That name Chubby fitted him just right. My mama was a real bitch loving on every puppy. She allowed us to play all day. At sunset, Mama and I saw Chubby off. We played all the way. Chubby disappeared into an enclosure so different from the jungle. It was so noisy and with so much activity that I was bewildered. Cattle lowing, chicken cackling, men talking, music blaring, etc.

Mama saw my confusion.

"On our way, Doggie," she said as she walked away. "He lives with human beings."

"Why not in the jungle?" I asked.

"His family won't survive the jungle," Mama explained. "They are very distant cousins of ours."

"What do they do with human beings?" I asked.

"I don't know," she said. "I've seen them walk together and play, and I am sure they eat together. They are often in the company of large herds of goats and cows."

I had so many questions, but Mama was in a hurry. She broke into a trot and I had to keep up.

That was then. I enjoyed every minute. Now I am alone. Mama never got to tell me what human beings do, but one thing I know is they caused her disappearance and that of my brothers. Human beings destroy, destroy, and destroy some more. I don't like them.

Indeed, the jungle is now uninhabitable. By day, the dozers raise gales of dust impeding all visibility. By night, there is no ground to forage. Every time I watch the dozers move, I wonder if they know full-blooded beings call the jungle home. I see them and run, but for how long will this be? How far will they go? I can't help thinking what came of the burrowers: the foxes, the hares, and the badgers. Buried in their holes? Senseless dozers, *utterly senseless.*

If not the dozers, hunger will kill me. A few days ago, at dusk, I made for Chubby's. It had been days since I'd had anything to eat. I hoped to get at least a morsel from an old friend. I prayed he would remember me. A real dog should. The earthmovers were silent, and the men were gone. I realized just how much of the jungle was gone too. The road was more paved than when we had walked with Mama. *My jungle,* I thought. I crept past a few men and finally came to Chubby's. Mama said, "You only go to human territory at night as they will be unable to positively differentiate you from their own dogs."

A hedge virtually sealed the enclosure. A noisy abode. Through an opening, I saw a cow, a goat, chickens, and men seated. I tried to make a dash for smallest of the animals but couldn't get past the briars with four-inch thorns on the hedge. They ripped me. I stifled a squeal. There was no getting past. The shrub was a kind I had never seen. Not jungle vegetation.

I perceived more than one dog, but there was none in sight. Then I saw a dugout spot in the ground. A perfect hideout for a dog. It was tempting to slump, but I didn't find peace. Suddenly, a loud, quirky bark came from the house. Four dogs came from nowhere and joined in the barking. Then there was the most deafening of noises: cackling chicken, lowing cattle, bleating sheep, and obviously startled men. An engine was ignited, but its drone was nothing like the dozers in the jungle.

I turned to run only to be stopped by someone's presence.

"What are you doing here?" came a loud whisper.

I nearly passed out. It was Chubby.

"I am hungry," I said.

"You aren't hunting here, are you?" he asked.

"Didn't see or hear you coming," I said softly. "Where were you?"

"See where the men were seated?" he replied. "I was seated at my master's feet when I saw you looking around. All the dogs have sensed you, and there are five of us. I am the oldest and can assure you I have the experience, but young dogs are enthusiastic to impress the boss with their sniff ability. Beware."

"Am I OK?" I asked.

"Don't worry," he said. "I am in charge." Indeed there was a sense of peace about him. He ran back to his master, went to every dog, and growled gently. Only a dog could understand he meant no cause for alarm. Just shut up. The dogs sat down but remained listless. They were baying for the intruder.

I moved farther down the hedge to avoid attracting more attention. The wind favored me.

In fact, aromas from the homestead were killing me.

Chubby's master was restless. He went into his house and came out with a light and a baton. Then he ordered the dogs to go with him. They were looking for the intruder. The dogs found me out, but every time they tried walking toward me, Chubby growled, derailing his master. He was most trusted so he carried the day.

Finding nothing, the team returned to the house. I was safe.

Chubby returned a little while later. "Now this is trouble," he said. "What brings you here?"

"I told you I am hungry," I said. "The jungle's empty."

"Good you didn't go any farther," he said. "I feared you'd gone to the chicken pen. I'd be ruined. Master would conclude I'd lost my skill."

"Where's the pen?" I asked.

"Just be afraid, very afraid," he said.

"Get me something to eat, brother," I begged.

"Give me five minutes," he said.

Chubby disappeared and returned with a bone the size of a weasel. I crushed it, swallowed, and felt like I'd had nothing.

"Is that all?" I asked.

"This is not the jungle," he said. "We have rations here. Do you hear a chime?"

Yes, I heard the chime.

"That's seven o'clock," he continued. "I must assist Master to get all the sheep into their pen. I'll be back at seven thirty. Don't go."

"I'll wait," I said. I had no idea what "seven o'clock" and "seven thirty" meant.

I watched Chubby and the other dogs run to their master. They wagged their tails as if in salute to a king. That annoyed me. I'd never do that to Simba, though I regarded him highly. Instead, I avoided him.

Master and beasts disappeared into a shed—the sheep pen, I guess. There was more bleating than cackling. I prayed some slaying was taking place. The exercise seemed to take an eternity.

When they came out, the man patted each dog on the neck, which they seemed to enjoy. Then the dogs sat in a circle, tongues and tails wagging. Another man brought out a large plate with a mountain of food and laid it before the dogs. They gobbled like I would have. I stifled a squeal. I paced restlessly in my little space. Fear kept me from leaping.

They waited to be served on a platter. Couldn't bring down a choice meal for themselves even in the midst of plenty: the chickens, the sheep, the goats, even the cats. How dumb. I drooled. Well, the food distracted them from me, and that was good for me.

The dogs left in five directions on the farm. Chubby came where I was. This must have been his spot.

"Anything for me?" I asked.

"We'll be going out," he replied. "That was barely enough for us."

"Why on a platter?" I asked.

"Etiquette," he replied. "It's a homestead, not the jungle."

"Why not get a lamb, a chicken for yourself?" I asked.

"Scratch a chicken at your own peril," he said.

"What?"

"The men will put you down," he said.

"What does that mean?" I asked.

"They'll kill you honorably. Besides, a shepherd dog is a beast of honor. He takes care of sheep and does not devour them."

"I'll be dead and buried before I watch a juicy sheep pass me by," I said.

"And you on your way out," he said. "You are nothing but skin and bone. Do you have offspring?"

"With who?" I asked. "You may be looking at the last wild dog." "On our way, cousin," he said.

We trotted away from the homestead. It was now pitch-dark and there were hardly any men on the path. Chubby explained that most men, including his master, would not be leaving their houses unless alarmed. Most nights were calm. We went past several homes on each side of the path.

"My former play and hunting grounds," I said.

"Consider joining us now," he said.

"To wag my tail at a man?" I asked him.

He didn't answer.

Farther down was a settlement with as many houses as there had been trees in the jungle. There had to be many more human beings here than in Chubby's home. I remember vividly when this was part of the jungle. The jungle is doomed.

This settlement had too much light for my comfort. There was no hedge but a concrete wall around it.

"Why the concrete wall?" I asked. "To keep out the likes of me?"

"No, to keep out other men," Chubby responded. "They wreak more havoc on one another than you and I would."

I was afraid. There was nowhere to hide. The glaring light was on us.

Chubby sensed my fear. "Keep your distance from the wall and you'll be fine," he said.

I, however, wanted to peer into the houses. The wall was long, the size of a few hunting grounds. At one point, I got curious, scaled the wall, and peeped. My eyes fell on those of a little white beast. I thought it was a cat. It looked at me and squealed.

"What's that?" I asked Chubby. He too had scaled the wall.

"We must leave," he said. "It's a dog."

"Really?" I insisted. "It walks like a dog and squeals like a dog but does not look like a dog."

"It smells like a dog," Chubby said. "It's a dog. I don't know what the men did to his coat. They call him a poodle." He laughed.

"What's he doing there?" I asked.

"Did you see his bed?" asked Chubby. "You complained about our platter. You should see his bowl. He hangs out with the cats. But instinct dies hard."

I was disgusted.

We moved on along the perimeter wall, a long stretch that could cover a vast hunting ground. A little past the end of the wall, a putrid, musty smell hit us. Large flies buzzed, certainly the most nourished one could find. The jungle was here: the hyena, the cheetah, the warthog, the jackal, and any scavenger I knew. They congregated here as if at a spa. For a moment, I thought I'd find my folks here. None. It broke my heart. I knew they were no more. Simba too was not there. I didn't expect him. A nemesis of men just like my kind, he gave them wide berth. The other animals are too dumb to care. I longed for fresh antelope meat, but there was no grazer in sight. Of course they didn't want to be anyone's fodder. They might be here by day when there were no predators.

Somehow, the presence of the jungle dwellers was reassuring and I moved closer. Everyone was busy, and no one bothered with his neighbor. It reminded me of the watering points where we used to meet daily without fail. All the jungle dwellers would be there, including cats, dogs, browsers, and grazers. The smells and gases filled my stomach. Wild dogs aren't scavengers; I longed for fresh meat to rip. Stale carcasses were all that was available. Simba, they say, will eat grass if he finds no meat. This was no grass. I couldn't get myself to indulge. I wondered what of good health anyone would be getting here.

I knew hyenas to be scavengers, but I didn't expect them to stoop this low. Raw filth. The rats, roaches, and any vermin you can think of. Then the flies, flies, and more flies. As for warthogs, they are just swine. They were home.

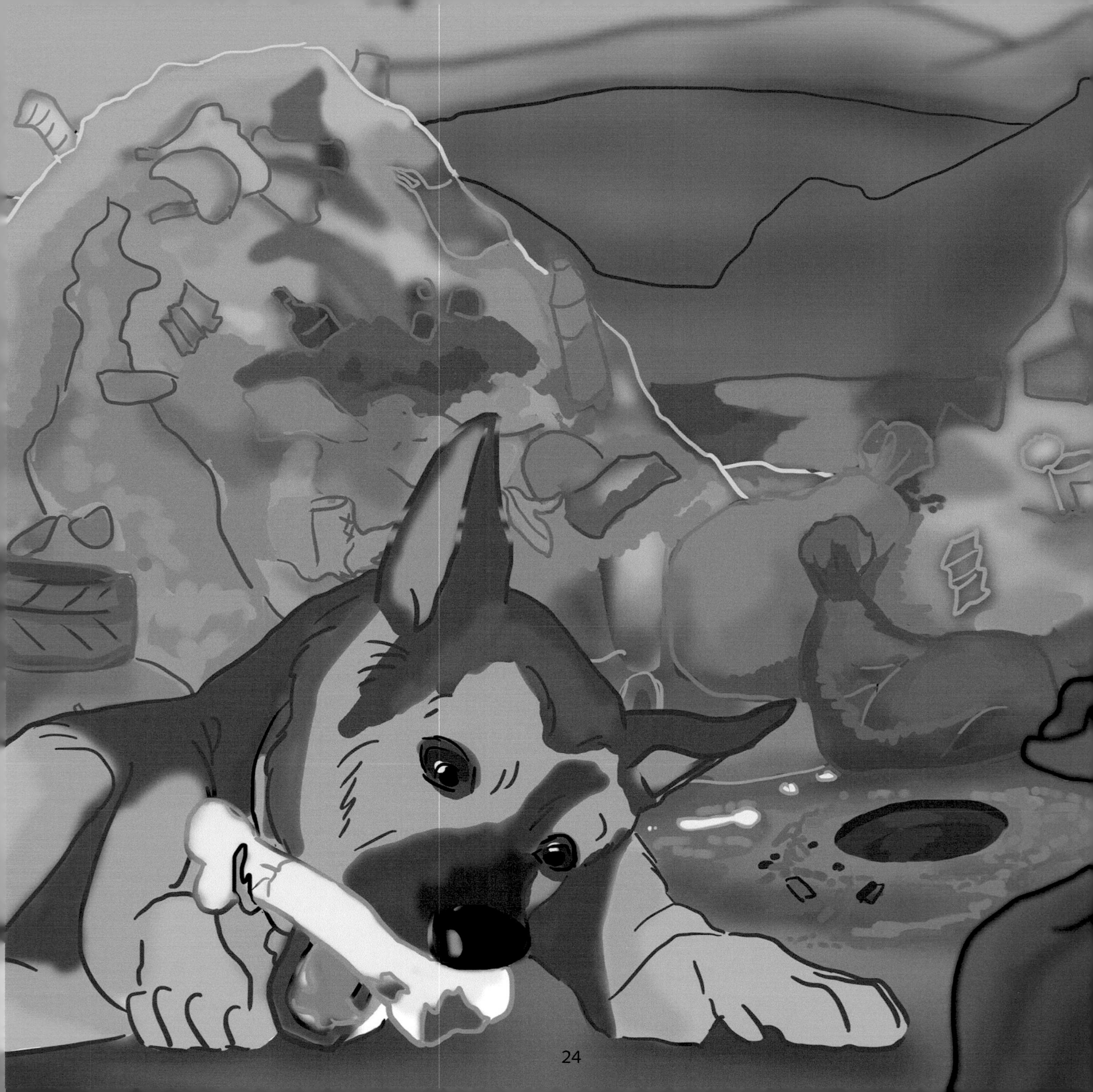

For a while, I stared at the scavenging beasts. I thought I lost Chubby. He had moved away and was gnawing at a large bone he'd found. He was unable to sink his dainty canines into the bone. His teeth had adjusted to mash on a platter. When I approached him, he growled as if he expected me to take away his find. Not me.

"You're not hungry," he said.

"Haven't you just eaten?" I asked.

"Was that enough for a bulldog?" he retorted.

"How do you stand all this?" I said.

"What everyone's doing," he said. "Soon you'll be an expert. Are you really hungry?"

"No thanks. I am blotted," I replied.

No, not today at least. I was hoping to run into a hare or squirrel on my way back. They haven't anywhere to hide. The dozers ruined their hideouts. I dreaded the day I would have to delve into the garbage.

I looked at the garbage again: paper, plastic, cloth, metal, glass, bone, ash in every form, complete cans and broken pieces, and every form of rubbish I would hate to see in the jungle. I doubt every animal was careful enough to avoid the broken pieces.

I strayed back toward the houses while hoping to find a cat or a young dog. A big bulldog pounced on me and growled. Then I heard the cries of men.

"It's a T9! A T9! A T9!" rang the voices.

I barely managed to snatch myself from the clutches of the big dog.

"Run for your life!" cried Chubby.

I took to my sore heels and made for the remaining jungle.

I did not know what a T9 was but figured it must be another name for a wild dog since I seemed to be the only one attracting attention. Only Chubby could tell me, but now we were running in different directions.

Mine may be the short life of the last wild dog, but only time will tell.

Printed in the United States
by Baker & Taylor Publisher Services